This book is dedicated to Jaime,
Melissa, and Denise.
These three women each have the heart
of a warrior.
They took on the challenge of hosting a five-day
camp for foster children.
My life has forever been changed because
of their unwavering determination to make a
difference.

Sunny Day Adventures

By Judy Pickrel
Illustrated by Charity Russell

CONTENTS

CHAPTER 1

GOODBYE ORDINARY

It was just an ordinary day until it became extraordinary. When the King wanted to meet with Lula and Todd, He would send one of His messengers to invite them to His banquet room. Today the King was walking right toward Lula and Todd. Had they forgotten an appointment? Had they forgotten to do something He had asked? They did not know why the King was approaching them, but they did know that anytime the King was involved they could say goodbye to the ordinary.

A mouse named Lula and a fire breathing dragon named Todd stood side by side. The King came closer until He was right in front of them with a grin as big as an upside-down rainbow. He looked into Lula and Todd's eyes and spoke. "In one week, I am sending you to a five-day camp for kids. You will be part of the staff." WHAT!? Now it was as if fireworks were set off in their minds. Every word burst in beautiful colors above their heads. "Camp, leave in one week, kids, five days, and staff." The

CAMP ONE WEEK
STAFF
KIDS
DAYS
5

King had never given them this much information about a mission. Now they knew who – kids. They knew what – camp. They knew when – one week. Then the King said, "We will meet at the castle gate at 9 a.m. one week from today." The King turned and left. Lula and Todd were like statues carved in stone unable to move.

Lula and Todd slowly regained their ability to move and think. The first thing they did was to try and figure out what the strange words "camp and staff" meant. They had no idea what camp was and wasn't a staff some kind of cane for old people? Lula and Todd asked everyone they saw if they knew the meaning of the words "camp and staff." No one knew what the human word "camp" meant. A few did know that the human word "cramp" could mean a pain in your leg so that might be why they would need a staff or a cane.

What kind of mission was this? Lula and Todd both thumped their foreheads and said "DUH." Who would know about camp and staff?   Professor Owl! They walked, which turned into a run, to ask Professor Owl what he knew about these peculiar sounding words, "camp and staff."

Professor Owl's eyes grew larger and larger like a balloon being filled with helium. His first words to Lula and Todd were, "You are in for the time of your life." He explained that camp was a special place for kids to get away from their ordinary routine and experience the extraordinary. The camp the King was sending them to was not just an ordinary camp - it was the "King's Camp." Staff had nothing to do with canes or old people. Staff meant adults, and now that would include a mouse and a fire breathing dragon, who would spend the week with kids and the goal was to have FUN, FUN, FUN!

Lula and Todd had no idea why the King would send them to camp with kids and the mission was to have fun, but they knew they could do that! This was nothing like any other mission the King had sent them on. Lula and Todd were excited but there was a lot to do to get ready and they were still not sure what was in store for them.

CHAPTER 2

DETAILS, DETAILS, DETAILS

The King told Lula she was to meet with the woman in charge of the camp. She would give Lula details on what she and Todd would need to bring. Lula still loved detailed plans. The King arranged for Lula to take a day trip to visit the lady in charge.

A mouse in the woman's kitchen on an ordinary Tuesday took the woman by surprise. Lula found herself being chased around the kitchen with a broom. She scampered behind the refrigerator to catch her breath and figure out a plan. How do you calm down a crazed woman with a broom? Lula slowly came out from behind the refrigerator with her hands in the air. The woman was shocked. What kind of mouse was this? A mouse standing on two hind legs with hands raised and then Lula spoke, "I am on a mission for the King." Those words spoken by a mouse in her kitchen on an ordinary Tuesday caused the woman to slowly melt like butter on a hot summer day onto the floor.

When she woke up Lula was on her left arm with a fan made from a lettuce leaf. The woman seemed to be nailed to the floor unable to move. Lula climbed up to the woman's ear and whispered, "I am on a mission for the King." The mention of the King calmed the woman, and she slowly sat up and for some unexplainable reason said, "Tell me how you met the King."

Lula began to tell her story. The woman quickly realized this was going to be a very long story and carried Lula to the kitchen table. She brought Lula cheese, crackers, and a plump purple grape. She then poured herself the biggest cup of coffee Lula had ever seen. Lula started at the beginning when she first discovered the door that led to the King.

Lula had gotten lost one day and discovered the most beautiful door she had ever seen. When Lula realized she was lost she panicked. After many wrong turns, she finally arrived back at her little mouse hole along the edge of the wall. As hard as she tried, she could not forget about the door. Lula decided to find the door again. It took some time, but one day she rounded the corner and there it was. That day changed her life forever. That day she discovered she was loved by the King.

Every day after that she had spent her time learning about the King and His Kingdom. On an ordinary Thursday, the King asked her to go into the dungeon and rescue Todd. Lula thought she would never be brave

enough to go into the dungeon and she had no idea who Todd was. Lula would trust the King. The King provided everything she needed to go on her first rescue mission. Finding Todd was a moment she would never forget. Todd was a fire breathing dragon. Every day she patiently sat and listened to Todd's story and then told him about the King. It took several days but one day Todd was ready to leave the dungeon and go meet the King. Lula and Todd became BFF's (Best Friends Forever) and now the King sent them to rescue others. The woman oohed and awed.

Now it was Lula's turn to take a seat and get comfortable. She began to nibble on the plump purple grape causing juice to run down her chin. The woman introduced herself. "Hi, my name is Mindy." Lula responded, "Hi, my name is Lula." Lula immediately knew she had connected with another BFF. Mindy was like a huge water fountain spewing words high in the air.

Mindy shared her story of being asked to go to the King's Camp to help with kids for a week and how it had changed her life. The King's camp was five fantabulous days of fun, fun, fun!

Mindy went on to tell Lula that the kids would fish, shoot arrows, and have a gigantic birthday party. They would swim, canoe, make crafts, and so much more. Mindy suddenly stopped in the middle of her story. Her face lit up like a search light that was now focused on Lula. She began to gesture wildly. The King wants you and Todd to tell the Bible story each day.

When the King had told Mindy He wanted Lula and Todd to be the Bible teachers she had no idea who that was. She never dreamed He meant a mouse and a fire breathing dragon. Now Lula was the one who melted like butter onto the floor. Lula woke up to see Mindy with a fan in her hand. Lula loved to tell others about the King one person at a time and teach large groups of animals. Now it seemed like the King wanted her and Todd to stand before a large group of humans and tell His story.

Professor Owl had long ago taught Lula and Todd the human language so there was no problem for Lula to share about the King. Still Lula felt the weed of fear she had known before she met the King begin to creep into her mind like a huge invading army. She had also learned how to stop weeds. She shouted, "I will trust the King."

It was as simple as that. This was the King's plan for her and Todd. He would give them everything they needed to share His story to humans.

CHAPTER 3

THE KING'S POWER PLANT

Lula spent all day with Mindy. She left with a long-detailed list of things to get ready for camp. Once back at the castle, Lula and Todd began to pack. They did not pack their helmets, belts of truth, or their shields of faith that they had taken on other rescue missions. Instead they packed water shoes, suntan lotion, casual clothes, and candy. Lots of candy that included bubble gum and taffy.

The most important thing to prepare was the Bible story. At camp Todd and Lula would tell a group of kids and adults the story of David and Goliath. For that to work, they would have to have the King's help. They were about to find out the King's provisions were limitless!

The King took them to another part of the castle they knew nothing about. It was a ginormous building with a sign over the door that read, "Power Plant." The huge, double doors were alive with living plants of every color and size. Some were tiny little sprouts and others were in full bloom. Part of the plants had fruit hanging from their branches.   Standing on either side of the majestic doors were Judy and Dennis. They were known as Master Gardeners throughout the Kingdom. Outside the door, Lula and Todd could hear voices of humans and animals inside. They heard lively music and singing. It sounded like a party was going on inside. Then with a nod from the King, Judy and Dennis swung open the doors.

Inside was a room beyond their wildest imagination. Lula's little beady eyes were now the size of a large pizza. Todd's normally large eyes were now the size of an enormous serving platter. What was this place? It was like a giant wonderland. Right in front of Lula and Todd were enormous containers made from priceless gems in every color of the rainbow. Every container overflowed with seeds. All around the containers were well worn paths. Behind the containers was a lush garden filled with every plant in the King's kingdom to produce more seeds. There was an endless supply. Lula and Todd knew these were not common ordinary seeds but extraordinary Kingdom seeds.

Beautiful horses pulled wagons filled with seeds to refill containers and more seeds to be planted. Lula and Todd jumped up and down when they spotted their friend Majesty pulling one of the wagons. Everyone sang with gusto as they worked for the King.

POWER PLANT

Again, the King looked right into Lula and Todd's eyes. With a smile now as big as the sky above the rainbow He said, "Take whatever seeds you want and take lots for those you will meet at camp." Professor Owl had taught them long ago the difference between weeds and seeds. Lula and Todd knew they needed to stay alert and not allow weeds to grow in their hearts. Weeds were completely opposite from Kingdom seeds. Weeds produced fear, hopelessness, anger, and other ugly things in their hearts. The King had always given them the Kingdom seeds they needed to destroy weeds. They could never have imagined that the King had an entire Power Plant filled with seeds.

Lula and Todd were like kids in a candy store who had just been told to go wild. They quickly realized these were the same seeds that the King gave them when the weeds of sadness or loneliness began to grow in their hearts. There were containers marked love, confidence, wisdom, hope and on and on. Inside these Kingdom seeds was the King's extraordinary power to free hearts of ugly weeds.

Lula knew immediately she would need more seeds of faith. She still had to fight the weed of fear when she did not have a long-detailed plan. She simply needed to have faith that the King had a plan. She was still afraid she could not speak in front of a large group of human adults and kids. As she walked down the path between the containers of seeds, her eyes locked on the smallest container labeled "Faith." It was made of pure gold.

Inside the container were itty bitty seeds. She knew from the past that it was possible for these tiny little seeds to produce a harvest of giant faith in her heart that would crush the weeds of fear. They reminded Lula of mustard seeds. She knew that if she had faith the size of one of these tiny seeds she could do anything the King asked. She took plenty for herself and even more to share.

Clear in the back of the Power Plant was a giant emerald container filled with huge seeds. Todd was not even convinced they were seeds. He made his way back to the container and saw the sign with the name of the seeds – "Patience." These seeds were at least twelve inches long and weighed a good forty pounds. According to the description these seeds could take 10 years to produce fruit.

They reminded Todd of the seeds in a double coconut. Coconut milk was one of Todd's favorite drinks, so Todd picked up two seeds. He loosened his belt of truth and squeezed in the seeds. One on each side. Todd knew from his past experience that he had doubted the King's love could change his life forever. Lula had been patient with him until he was ready to leave the dungeon and meet the King. Patience was the seed he needed to crush the weeds of doubt in the hearts of kids at camp.

Lula and Todd walked among the priceless containers. They scooped up seeds they would plant in the hearts of staff and campers. They added seeds of peace and kindness to their bags. They loaded up on seeds of friendship and courage. Dennis and Judy drove the wagon pulled by Majesty. It stopped next to Lula and Todd so they could load their bags in the back of the wagon.

Lula and Todd knew the Kingdom seeds of love had changed their lives forever. Now they could not wait to watch as the King allowed them to plant His life changing seeds of love in others. Kingdom seeds would destroy the lying weeds that made kids feel they were unloved. The King told them that the Power Plant was open day and night. All they had to do was let Nigel know, and he would make a "special delivery" of anything they needed.

Once back in their rooms, Lula and Todd quickly realized that they had a lot of things to take with them. On other missions they took almost nothing. The King provided for them as they went. Now they were to take everything they needed with them. Would Mindy have room for everything? Suddenly Lula remembered Mindy had told her that if she had any questions the King's carrier pigeon named Nigel would bring a message to her and she would send back a reply. The King had also just told them about Nigel. They had to find Nigel fast!

Nigel lived at the King's castle, but Lula had never met him. She discovered that when a message could not be delivered on land by Ollie the Ostrich, Nigel would take to the air. When Nigel saw Lula approaching with an envelope, he knew to get ready to leave. By the time Lula stood in front of him he had put on a leather helmet with goggles. Around his waist was a belt of truth. A bag marked "Air Mail" hung down from his belt. Nigel did not waste any time. He read the address on the envelope and placed it in his bag. Before Lula knew what had happened, Nigel was in the air. As he flew higher and higher, she heard him tweet "Tootle Loo."

Before the sun set, Mindy had sent Nigel back with the answer. "No worries!" There was plenty of room in the trucks, trailers, vans, and a bus they would take to camp. Lula liked that Mindy and her team had taken care of all the details. Now Lula and Todd needed to make sure they packed everything on Lula's very long list of things to take and try to get some sleep.

CHAPTER 4

PACKED AND READY TO GO

Lula woke up even earlier than her usual 4:30 a.m. Todd was already up and had packed everything they would need. Today they would leave for camp. Just as the King had instructed, Lula and Todd met Him at the castle gate at exactly 9 a.m. with all their supplies. The King gave Todd the GPS coordinates for the church where the team would meet. So far, the only thing that was ordinary about this mission was Lula flew to the top of Todd's head using the wings of love the King had given her a long time ago and snuggled down. She carried a small pouch of faith seeds with her. The rest of the faith seeds were packed with all the other seeds. Bag after bag of seeds and other supplies were tied to Todd. Todd raised his wings to their full width of six feet. Then with a mighty push downward, Todd and Lula were off to join the camp team.

Todd was thankful the church was only a short distance away. Bags were hung from his tail, tied to his

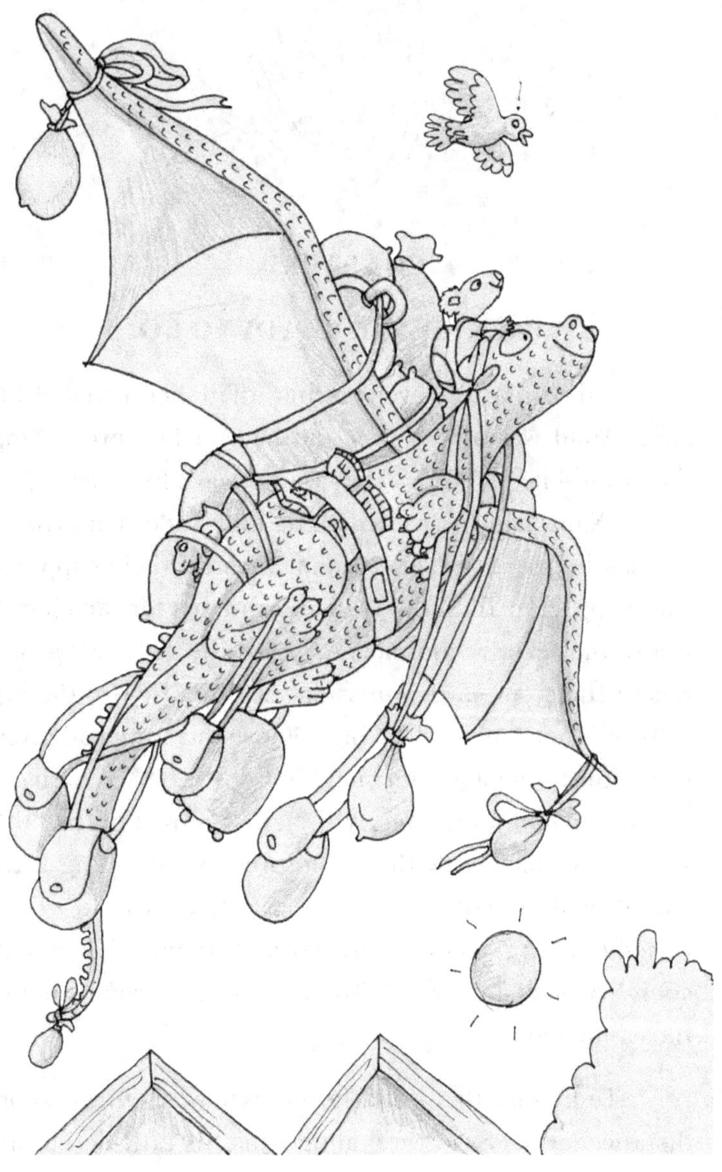

wings, draped around his neck, and hanging from his feet. He had two giant seeds of patience shoved into his belt. Because of the weight, Todd was not able to fly very high. He flew just high enough to barely get over the tops of houses. Todd now thought they may have gone overboard on the candy. People shouted and dogs howled as Lula and Todd made their way to the church.

The entire team was to meet at the church. Todd and Lula landed in the church parking lot. The look on the greeter's face was priceless. The fact that the dragon looked like a flying moving van made the sight less frightening. The greeter could not help but laugh. He quickly helped Lula and Todd find where to takc all their supplies. He then took them inside the church. As he was ushering Lula and Todd in, others cleared out an entire section of chairs just for Lula and Todd.

It was like a huge current of electricity flowed through the church. Everyone smiled, gave high-fives, and talked excitedly. There were whispers about a fire breathing dragon and a mouse joining the team going to camp. That only added to the excitement of what the King had in store for them. After everyone had arrived at the church and all the supplies loaded, they were ready to leave.

Cars, vans, trucks, and a bus left the church parking lot. There were boxes and boxes of supplies the staff members would need. There were huge containers marked "crafts." There were fishing poles, first aid kits, and lots and lots of snacks. Along with the boxes Lula and Todd had brought for the Bible story, they had loaded their precious seeds. It was like watching a freight train pull out of a train station. What a week this was going to be. Fun, food, and friends would all make for five fantabulous days. Lula and Todd followed the train below from high above.

After a short time, the train of cars, vans, trucks, and a bus pulled onto the camp site. Lula and Todd could see the lake as they flew over. They spotted the swimming pool and the building where they would eat their meals. From down below one of the team members pointed out where Lula and Todd would tell the kids the story of David and Goliath. Lula and Todd landed in front of the building where the kids would stay.

Everyone pitched in and quickly unloaded the cars, vans, trucks, and a bus. They looked like a large colony of ants carrying supplies in every direction. Even when everything was unloaded, there was still work to be done. The staff was divided into groups to help with crafts, those who would stay in rooms with the kids, those who would help with group activities and then there were the whatever is needed staff. Lula and Todd were part of the "whatever is needed" staff.

At the King's castle there was a group called the Crafty Critters. The King's camp had their own group of crafty humans who began to make signs with the name of each kid who would come to camp. Glitter filled the air. Those who would be staying in rooms with kids found their room. Posters and banners went up on the walls. There was no doubt this was going to be five fantabulous days. It was like Christmas Eve. All the staff went to sleep as the words, "The kids are coming! The kids are coming!" danced in their heads.

In the morning one staff member was on lookout duty. He had a walkie talkie to stay connected with the driver of the bus loaded with kids headed to camp. The ETA (estimated time of arrival) was counted down. Finally, Lula and Todd heard the shout go up "The kids are here!"

CHAPTER 5

CAMP OFFICIALLY BEGINS

The staff could not stand still. They waved, cheered, and jumped up and down as the big bus rolled to a stop. Lula flew to the top of Todd's head to avoid being accidently stepped on. Once she was safe, she began to wave and cheer with the rest of the staff. Then the bus doors opened. Jaime held a megaphone and announced the first camper's name - Mandy. Kaitlyn held the poster with Mandy's name high in the air and cheered. Thirty campers in all came off the bus and walked down the red carpet. Camp had officially begun.

Todd noticed one little girl who got off the bus kept her head down. She did not make eye contact with anyone. Out of all the extraordinary kids that got off the bus, Todd was drawn to the one little girl who kept her head down and tried to go unnoticed. His hand reached down and held one of the seeds of patience tucked into his belt.

Minutes later a boy named Peter jumped off the bus and ran down the red carpet. He threw papers at everyone and yelled. Lula just smiled. She remembered how Todd had acted when she first met him. Everyone had been scared of Todd because he could breathe fire. Lula was determined to get to know Peter. The King had completely changed Todd and she knew the King would do the same for Peter. She was thankful for her seeds of faith.

After lunch it was time for the campers to find their rooms and see where they would stay for the next four days. Each room was decorated and ready when kids ran inside with their bags. Lula found her name posted on a door along with five girls. Wendy was the staff person who would be staying in her room. Lula could not wait to meet Wendy and the five girls who would be staying in her room.

She scurried inside the room and immediately scampered up on a top bunk. She made her way to the bottom of the bed and laid out the shredded paper she had brought to make her nest. As she made her nest, a girl named Mary quietly climbed up and put her things on the bed. When Mary saw Lula, she quickly made sure not to come near Lula's nest.

It was clear right from the beginning that Todd was TOO big to stay in one of the rooms. It was decided that Todd would be the night security guard. He would make sure that nothing happened that would scare any of the kids. Todd loved being the security guard. He quickly found Peter's room. Everyone was scared of Peter and stayed away from him. Todd chuckled. Peter acted just like he used to act.

The kids could not believe there was a fire breathing dragon at camp. They quickly discovered that Todd was friendly. Several kids would sit on his tail, and he would lift them off the ground and swing them from side to side. Every kid screamed, "more, more!" A few were even more adventurous and climbed to the top of Todd's head. They could see out over the entire campground. Everyone loved Todd right from the beginning.

The little girl Todd had watched get off the bus with her head down stayed a safe distance away from everyone. Her name was Mary. He was glad he had two seeds of patience. One for Mary and one for Peter. Todd knew there were weeds growing in Mary and Peter's hearts. He also knew that Kingdom seeds would change them forever. He just needed to be patient.

Lula spotted Peter. He was still causing trouble, and everyone stayed away from him. Out of all the extraordinary kids at camp, Lula was sure that she would become best friends with Peter and her bunk mate, Mary. The staff was ready to make sure every child had a week they would never forget, but wondered if what they did in five days could last a lifetime. Lula told them about the

King's seeds they had brought to plant into their hearts and the hearts of the kids.

Bags of seeds now hung all over Todd. There were seeds of bubbling joy, laughter already beginning to erupt, and the bag of hope floated high over Todd's head. Staff swarmed Todd like bees on honey. They now had seeds they would ask the King to plant in their own hearts and even more seeds to plant in the hearts of kids. Some still wondered if Kingdom seeds could really change a life forever. Did Kingdom seeds really have the power to destroy weeds? Lula and Todd never doubted. The seed of faith had grown tall and strong in their hearts.

CHAPTER 6

A WILD RIDE

Morning - for some it was glorious and for some it would be glorious in another five to six hours. Some bounced out of bed like kangaroos. Some rolled out like slow turtles. But breakfast was at 8 a.m. so everyone was on the move.

Lula and Todd were thrilled to find breakfast was a feast that reminded them of the King's banquet table. There were biscuits covered in gravy and cinnamon rolls the size of dinner plates. The food was definitely provided by the King. Todd noticed everyone was excited about the day ahead except for Mary who sat at a table for eight, but did not join in any of the excited chatter.

Across the room Lula saw Peter still causing trouble. Everyone stayed a safe distance away from him. Lula scurried over to his table and scrambled up the table leg. Peter saw her and threw a biscuit at her head. Lula, quick as a lightning bolt, put up her paws and grabbed the biscuit out of the air. Peter just glared at her while the other boys at the table exploded in laughter.

Right after breakfast, there was always a time of celebration. The kids were taught new Kingdom songs with great dance moves. Then it was time for Lula and Todd to tell the Bible story about David. Lula and Todd both remembered their trip to the King's Power Plant and knew the King had already given them everything they needed. Lula stepped out on the stage with no fear! The seeds of faith had forced out the weeds of fear. The seeds of courage the King had planted in her filled her from the top of her head all the way through her tiny little toes.

Lula told the kids David was a little boy that no one noticed or expected do anything great. David's job was to watch sheep eat grass all day. He had seven older brothers who took care of all the important work. Three of the seven were even a part of the King's army. His brothers told David he was not important and was only able to watch sheep. His brothers planted weeds of loneliness and doubt that he would ever do anything great in his heart. The kids at camp knew about not being noticed. No one thought they would do great things. They often felt alone like David. They had those same weeds growing in their hearts.

Todd was in the back and noticed the little girl named Mary nodded her head. She knew exactly how it felt to feel hidden in plain sight. Todd was still determined that by the end of the week he would be best friends with Mary and with the boy named Peter. Todd no longer carried the seeds of patience in his belt, he had asked the King to plant them in his heart.

Miss Mindy had made a long-detailed schedule. She had divided up the kids into different activities along with staffers to help. The first morning Lula was assigned to fishing. She had never been fishing, and truth be told, she was not fond of water or worms. But she would do whatever was asked of her.

Darrell oversaw fishing and knew everything fishy. He was ready with fishing poles and worms when a gaggle of girls ran his way. He quickly handed out poles and directed staffers to put worms on hooks. Lula was asked to guard the worm can. She made sure to put it in a safe place so no worms would escape. One of the girls let out a shrill shriek and Lula turned to see what had happened. She had caught her FIRST FISH EVER!

Lula had looked away for only a moment but in that split second someone had kicked over the worm can. Worms were on the loose. Lula had no idea a fat worm could wiggle so fast. They were like runners at a track meet, and they were off. All the staffers and girls ran to help Lula surround the runaway worms to make sure none escaped. Lula chased after one especially speedy worm. The worm had the grassy area ahead in sight. Lula was like a long jumper and leapt close to twenty inches and

landed on top of the worm. She quickly wrapped her arms around the worm and held on like a cowboy on a bucking bronco. The worm was racing to freedom carrying Lula along with him.

Fortunately for Lula, one of the staffers spotted her and came to her rescue. She picked up Lula along with the worm. She separated the two and placed the squirmy worm back in the can. The tragedy of Lula being carried away by a giant worm was stopped. Victory cheers filled the air. Stories of how Lula rode a giant worm spread like wildfire.

As the story was passed from girl to girl, the worm got bigger and bigger and Lula's ride even more amazing. Lula, however, was quiet as she puzzled over how the accident could have happened. She had made sure the can was in a safe place. She wondered if someone had deliberately kicked the can over and why would someone do that?

The rest of the time at the lake went by without incident. Every girl caught a fish. Lula smiled as she watched staffers gently plant seeds of the King's love into the hearts of campers. Lula knew love had the power to change everything. However, the nagging thought about someone deliberately upsetting the can of worms was still bothering her.

CHAPTER 7

BULLSEYE

The boys had been assigned to archery. They heard the commotion from the fishing area, and they were not to be out done by the girls. When someone hit a bullseye, it sounded like they had won a major sporting event as they whooped and hollered. The shouts from the fishing area and the shouts from archery mixed together to make one giant sound like hundreds of cymbals being clashed together.

The girls gathered up all the fishing stuff and talked about when it would be their turn at archery. None of the girls had ever shot a bow and arrow. Archery would be another "first time" experience. They could hardly wait. Then they heard the boys go wild. What was going on?

The girls ran to the staffers and Darrell. Everyone wanted to know what in the world had happened at the archery range. They all ran! It was like a stampede of runaway cattle. It is hard to believe but Darrell led the way. They went single file over a little bridge and ran up a hill. The archery range was in full view. At first, they did not see any reason for all the wild yelling. Then they looked further up the hill, and they saw the reason for the commotion–TODD!

Todd was marching down the hill dressed like a warrior going into battle. He had on a helmet, a belt, a huge sword hanging at his side, and size twenty-six camouflage combat boots. Unlike a warrior headed into battle, Todd grinned ear to ear. Now everyone let out a cheer for Todd. They began to chant, "Todd! Todd! Todd!"

When Todd arrived at the archery range, the boys ran to find a bow and arrow for him to shoot. The bows were like tiny toys and the arrows like matchsticks compared to Todd. Just when everyone thought Todd would not be able to shoot a bow and arrow, up drove James on a four-wheeler.

James had heard that the boys would be at the archery range and Todd wanted to join them. Long into the night he had worked to make a bow from a hickory tree branch the perfect size for Todd. He had found straight sticks for arrows and turkey feathers so the arrow would fly straight. The bow was strung with a purple nylon cord. It seemed impossible but Todd's grin continued to grow bigger and bigger. He stepped up in front of the target and placed an arrow on the purple nylon cord.

Truth

Todd pulled the string all the way back, aimed, and the arrow flew straight to the target. BULLSEYE! All the girls, boys, and staffers whooped and hollered.

It was so loud that the lunchroom staffers ran to the archery range to see what had happened. Lula then noticed something move behind the rack of arrows and she thought she heard someone whisper Peter's name. Lula watched Peter then head for the rack filled with arrows. He grabbed a handful of arrows and was ready to throw them. James gently took the arrows and placed them back in the rack. The Kingdom seed of kindness had been sown into Peter's heart.

Lula was puzzled who would hide behind the rack of arrows? Who had whispered Peter's name and why? Was someone trying to plant weeds (words that were not Kingdom seeds) in Peter's heart. Lula was now sure someone had deliberately kicked over the can of worms. She wondered if whoever whispered to Peter was the same person who kicked over the can of worms. Could there be more than one person trying to plant weeds in the hearts of campers?

After everyone settled down, Todd led the entire camp back up the hill to the dining hall. They were all starved after the morning adventures. Todd was shocked when he saw Mary come and walk right beside him. Todd invited her to climb up his scales and sit on top of his head. Mary did not waste a minute and climbed to the top of Todd's head. For the first time in Mary's life, she felt special. Wendy wondered if the Kingdom seed of truth that she was special would continue to grow when she left camp?

After a quick lunch, the kids spotted Grandpa and Grandma. Grandpa and Grandma always had candy and even more important than candy, Grandpa and Grandma had smiles, hugs, and Kingdom seeds of encouragement that they planted in every child every time. Every seed of encouragement pushed out weeds of discouragement that had been spoken to the child.

Out of the corner of Todd's eye he saw someone with Peter. It was not a staffer and not one of the camp kids. Todd began to walk toward Peter. Just then Peter crowded in and grabbed a handful of candy. Grandpa simply held out his hand and said, "Here Peter have one more piece." Peter was quiet for just a moment and then left. Grandpa grinned knowing he had planted the King's seed of generosity and it would spread like a watermelon vine overpowering any weeds. The person who had been with Peter was gone. Todd knew someone had tried to plant a weed of greed in Peter's heart. Todd knew greed was NOT a Kingdom seed. He would be on the lookout.

All afternoon some of the kids and staff swam and others made a bee line to the craft room. The camp crafters had brought tube after tube of glitter in every color. It was as if a glitter bomb went off in the craft room.

Darrell sparkled from head to toe.   By mid-day it was amazing to watch as the morning kangaroos turned into turtles and the morning turtles turned into kangaroos. Who knew there was a kangaroo and a turtle inside each person!

As another day ended, Lula and Todd found a quiet place and shared what they had seen. Now they both knew someone, or more than one person, had tried to plant weeds into the hearts of campers. Todd and Lula were now on high alert.

CHAPTER 8

LET THE SHENANIGANS BEGIN

Up and down the hallways you could hear the calls of "Rise and Shine." Once again, the morning kangaroos and turtles were up, dressed, and headed to breakfast. After an enormous breakfast, everyone was ready for another great day at camp.

The kids were now into the routine. It was time to sing songs to the King and find out what was happening to David. Lula told the kids David's brothers did not think David would ever do anything great and planted weeds of discouragement in his heart. They did not know God had planted seeds of greatness in David. David had potential. She told the kids that the King had planted seeds of greatness and potential in every one of them and in every staffer. The King's seed of courage continued to grow bigger and bigger inside Lula's heart as she stood in front of a room full of humans.

The kids could hardly wait to see what was on the

day's schedule. High-fives were given as one group would spend the morning in canoes and one group would spend the morning in the swimming pool. The groups would switch for the afternoon. Lula and Todd were both super excited about being assigned to canoes. It would be the first time for Todd and Lula to be on a lake.

At 10 a.m. Lula and Todd headed down to the water. Todd immediately spied Jimmy. He was the staff person for Peter's room. All the kids still avoided Peter. Todd quickly joined Jimmy and the two of them acted silly and did whatever the kids wanted to do. The two motioned for Peter to join them, and he did! From that moment on they were like three peas in a pod. The seed of friendship was taking root in Peter's heart.

Everyone was gathered at the dock where the kids had fished the day before. The beach was now filled with canoes about to be filled with kids. Todd immediately ran to a canoe and pushed it out into the water. Todd and the canoe sank like a rock. Peter and Jimmy jumped into the lake like superheroes to help Todd get on his feet. They pulled the canoe back to shore. The three joined hands and bowed to the crowd. Cheers filled the air.

The camp crafters sprang into action. They found a huge innertube and attached ropes of all different lengths. Todd stepped into the middle. They then told Todd to walk into the water. When he got out far enough that he could not touch the bottom of the lake, they showed him how to paddle his feet. Todd became a floating fun center. Kids went ballistic. They swam to Todd's tail and climbed up.

To everyone's surprise Peter quietly made sure everyone went in an orderly line. The seeds of kindness were continuing to grow bigger and bigger. Kids climbed up Todd's spikes to the top of his head and then jumped off. Mary was sitting on the edge of an inner tube with her feet dangling in the water. A staff member swam underwater and began pulling her toes. Mary did not move and thought a fish was nibbling her toes. Just then the staffer popped her head out of the water, and everyone was in hysterical laughter. Mary laughed the hardest.

Mary and Peter were now both having the time of their lives. Every staff member was thrilled that each child was having a great time at camp, but the question was still, "what about when they had to leave?" Could Kingdom seeds get rid of the weeds in their hearts when they went home? Lula made sure to plant seeds of faith in every staffer's heart.

Peter and Jimmy were ready to get in a canoe and paddle out into the middle of the lake. They put on their life jackets and slowly got in their canoe. It was a little tricky because the canoe rocked back and forth but they helped one another and off they went. One by one canoes were pushed out onto the lake.

The crafters had made sure to make Lula a lifejacket

and she took her place at the very front of the canoe. She stood up on the bow of the boat and spread out her arms. The water was as smooth as silk as they glided across the calm lake further and further from the shore.

As the canoers were headed back to shore, Jimmy and Pastor Steve got into a water war. They dipped their paddles into the water. At the exact same time they brought their paddles up out of the water. Water flew everywhere. Staff and campers were soaked. No one ever really knew how it happened but all of a sudden Pastor Steve and his canoe were upside down in the water.

Everyone held their breath. Then Pastor Steve burst out of the water like a rocket headed for the moon. He began to swim towards Jimmy and Peter. They paddled like two busy beavers back to shore. The other canoers went crazy with laughter. This was a day everyone would remember. The seeds of joy had begun to bubble up and laughter erupted everywhere.

The afternoon meant everyone switched. The canoers would swim, and the swimmers would head to the canoes. That meant fun at the pool for Lula and Todd. The camp crafters had helped the kids make a small boat out of aluminum foil for Lula. They made sure that Lula had on her life jacket and helped into her own boat. Lula was like the captain of her own little ship as she floated through the water. Todd was Todd. Right in the middle of everything.

Kids were climbing on him. Kids were hanging on his tail as he swung them side to side like water skiers. Lula suddenly flew to the top of Todd's head. Todd carried Lula down to the deep end of the pool as if she were the Captain of a great ship. Every boy and girl got a turn to climb to the top of Todd's head as he carried them through the water like great sea captains.

As the kids got ready for bed, word spread through every room like spilled milk on a kitchen floor about a birthday party the next day. Several of the kids had never had their very own birthday party and could hardly wait to see what was planned for the next day. Lula snuggled down in her nest at the bottom of Mary's bed dreaming about the birthday party. Lula had never had her own birthday party. Mary poked her head down to the end of the bed and invited Lula to move her bed up by her pillow. Lula almost squealed for joy but did not want to wake everyone. Lula made her way to Mary's pillow and snuggled next to Mary's ear. The Kingdom seed of friendship was sprouting in Mary's heart pushing out the weeds of loneliness.

Todd was on night patrol and overheard staffers talking about the big party the next day. He overheard as Peter asked Jimmy if he would be included in the party. Todd understood how Peter felt. There was a time that Todd was never included in anything. Todd grinned when he heard Jimmy say "Yes, Peter we are celebrating your birthday tomorrow." Todd smiled as the boy went from being filled with the weed of anger to allowing the Kingdom seed of hope to float higher and higher. That very thing had happened to Todd a long time ago when Todd met the King. Todd knew the change in Peter's heart would last forever.

CHAPTER 9

THE BATTLE OF WEEDS AND SEEDS

The kids were excited about the big birthday party and were up early. The kangaroos were up and bouncing twice as high as normal. Even the kids who were normally morning turtles were all keeping pace with the kangaroos. However, part of the staffers were slow to get going even for turtles. When everyone in the room was ready, they headed to the dining hall and breakfast.

With everyone's tummy full, a line formed to go to celebrate the King and hear more of the David and Goliath story. The sound of music filled the air. They could not wait to get started. Anyone who wanted to go to the front and help lead songs ran up front. Kids from every part of the room headed to the front pulling a staff person with them. Now there were no staffers. Everyone was a kid. The fruit of the King's seed of joy and laughter could be heard everywhere. Lula and Todd told the kids more about David. Now they could choose what they wanted to do.

The day was less scheduled which allowed the kids to go back to their favorite activities. It was like fallen leaves scattered by a strong wind. Kids and staffers headed every direction. Some went to archery aiming for one more bullseye. Some wanted one more canoe ride and others found Darrell with dreams of catching "The Big One." At last, it was time to clean up, rest and then get ready to PARTY!

Even though this was rest time no one could rest. Lula was settled in on Mary's pillow. Mary sat on the edge of her bed and watched the other girls from a distance. She was holding a piece of paper in her hand. Lula made her way to Mary's side and sat down. Mary handed the paper to Lula. It said, "no gifts for you." Someone had snuck into their room to plant weeds of discouragement and sadness in Mary's heart. Lula took the paper and tore it into a million pieces. She then climbed up onto Mary's shoulder and told Mary not to believe what was written on the paper. The words were weeds meant to make Mary cry. Lula promised there would be gifts for Mary. Lula was now hopping mad and determined to find out who was planting weeds and put a stop to it!

Finally party time arrived, and everyone was like a kangaroo and made their way to the party area. There were NO turtles. As the kids got close to the outdoor party area, they were speechless. There was a cotton candy machine, popcorn, and blue snow cones. All you could eat and FREE. Once again you could not tell staffers from kids. Everyone had blue snow cone lips as they filled their mouths with pink fluffy cotton candy.

An announcement was made for everyone to come under the giant pavilion and sit at one of the picnic tables. When everyone was at a table, staffers carried in tray after tray of decorated birthday cakes. Each child had their own cake with their name written on top in yummy icing. Mary was the first one to get her own birthday cake. Lula almost fell off Mary's shoulder when a staffer brought a cake with "Lula" in bright neon pink frosting. This was Lula and Mary's first time to have their own birthday cake.

Todd got a very large cake with a giant candle on top. Every eye was glued on Todd. They all wanted to see Todd breath fire. Todd looked around the room to find Mindy. She nodded her head up and down. Todd sucked in a tiny whisp of air and held it. Everyone there held their breath. With one quick little puff, fire came out of Todd's mouth and lit the candle. An explosion of cheers followed.

Then in came James on his four-wheeler. Behind the four-wheeler was a wagon filled with huge party bags. Peter beamed like a full moon. Mary grinned ear to ear. Wrapping paper began to fly and shouts of joy filled the entire campground as each child opened gifts that had been bought just for them. Every child knew that day that the King had chosen them to be His child and He loved

HAPPY BIRTHDAY
Todd
Lula
Mary
Jack

them. That was especially true for Mary. It was fantastic to watch the King's seeds of joy, laughter, and hope that had been planted all week-long burst through and fill the air. Lula motioned for Todd and told him about the note Mary had found on her bed. Someone was definitely trying to plant weeds. But who?

Pastor Steve put out a challenge for a cannon ball contest off the diving board. Everyone headed to the pool. The winner would be whoever was able to splash the most water on everyone in the pool and everyone along the edge of the pool. A long line of girls, boys, and staffers formed to take on the challenge.

A panel of judges sat on the side of the pool ready to score each leap off the diving board. A score of "10" was for a perfect splash. Contestant after contestant walked to the end of the diving board and hurled themselves into the water. Part of the jumpers pulled up their knees, others held their nose and ran off the end of the board at breakneck speed. Pastor Steve was feeling confident the winning trophy would be his.

Just as the contest was down to only a few, Peter noticed a little boy on the edge of the pool looking sad. Daniel was in Peter's room and Peter knew Daniel missed his family. Daniel was thin, small for his age, and would barely make any splash when he jumped in the water. Peter began to motion for Todd.

Todd would not have believed the change in Peter,

but the very same thing had happened to him. The Kingdom seed of caring for others had taken root in Peter's heart. Todd made his way around the edge of the pool and got close to Daniel and whispered in his ear. Daniel lit up like a neon sign on a starless night. He began to climb up the spikes on Todd's back until he reached the very top of Todd's head. Todd then made his way to the line at the diving board. Everyone froze. What was going on? Pastor Steve turned white as a sheet. He knew his trophy was in danger.

Then it was Todd and Daniel's turn. Todd edged his way to end of the board not sure it would hold the weight of a dragon and a boy named Daniel. Todd did not think it was wise to push his luck and did not jump on the board but simply stepped off the end. Daniel let out a shout "GERONIMO" that shocked everyone. No one expected that shout to come from tiny little Daniel.

When Todd and Daniel hit the water, it caused a gigantic wave that swept to the other end of the pool drenching everyone with water. As everyone was recovering, the wave floated back, and everyone in the pool and those sitting on the edge of the pool were soaked for a second time. The judges all held up perfect "10's" and declared Daniel the canon ball champ. Pastor Steve ran to Todd and Daniel giving high-fives. Peter stood on the edge of the pool as Todd swam up and gave him a high-five. There was no doubt kingdom seeds were more powerful than weeds.

CHAPTER 10

A GIANT PROBLEM

The last day of camp felt like two huge armies colliding. Everyone talked about all the fun they had during the week. The size of the fish they caught got bigger every time they told their story. The story of Lula on the back of a giant worm had turned into a heroic feat of bravery. The three peas in a pod were now legends. Everyone had changed. Along with the celebration of a great week there was the reality that everyone had to go home. Would the King's seeds continue to grow in the hearts of kids and staffers or would weeds take over when they went home?

The kids filed in one last time to celebrate the King with their songs. After the songs, wild dancing, and laughter the kids quickly settled into their seats. The lights went down. It was time for Lula and Todd to finish the story about the little shepherd boy named David. Lula played the part of David.

David was a shepherd, so Lula was dressed in simple everyday clothes wearing a backpack and carrying a slingshot. David's father had sent David to check on his brothers who were camped on a hillside across from their enemies. He came bringing food and other supplies from home for his three brothers.

Lula walked across the stage carrying a backpack filled with supplies. When she reached center stage, a voice boomed over the speaker system, "Send someone out to fight me. Winner takes all." It was Goliath. Lula continued to tell the story. "Goliath was on the other side of the valley. He was part of the enemies camp. Goliath stood over nine feet tall. He wore the armor of a warrior. His head was covered by a helmet. His chest and legs covered with armor. A huge sword hung from Goliath's belt."

The challenge from Goliath was for one man from David's country of Israel to fight him and whoever won would take the other side as prisoners. From the back of the room, Todd came out wearing full armor. A hush fell over the room. Who would be willing to fight a giant? No one in King Saul's army was brave enough to fight Goliath one on one. Not one of David's brothers volunteered. Not even King Saul.

From the stage Lula continued to play the part of David and spoke in a loud and confident voice, "I will fight Goliath." David's brothers were embarrassed and angry. Here was their little brother ready to fight Goliath. David was a shepherd boy and not trained as a soldier. How could a skinny little kid like David fight a giant? No one there expected David to ever do anything great. No one ever noticed David. He was just the kid who took care of the sheep as they ate grass. But David knew the King had planted seeds of greatness in him. David was the only one who volunteered. He was taken to King Saul.

Lula told the kids King Saul did not think David's odds of winning were good. In fact, King Saul did not think David had any chance to win the battle with Goliath, but David was his only choice. King Saul quickly had his armor brought for David. Lula tried to hold up a huge helmet. It looked like a giant swimming pool compared to Lula and not something she could use to protect her head. She tried to wear combat boots and fell inside and then scrambled out. Everything was too big and too heavy.

Lula brought out a small sling shot and five smooth stones from her backpack and said the words David had spoken to Goliath, "I will come against Goliath in the name of the King with my slingshot and these five smooth stones." Just then Mary stood to her feet and yelled, "Go Lula."

Again, Goliath's voice boomed over the speaker system like rippling thunder across the entire room as

Todd moved closer. Lula walked slowly down the stage steps. From the other side of the chapel Todd took three steps closer. Not the fun-loving Todd the kids had played with all week. Todd was now acting like Goliath.

He carried a huge dragon size sword. A helmet big enough for Lula and all her friends to swim in. The look on Todd's face was fierce. All the kids were on their feet so they could see tiny Lula with a sling shot. Every child there knew what it felt like to face a giant problem. The truth was every adult knew that feeling too.

As David (Lula) stood facing Goliath (Todd) she told the kids that David knew that the King was with him. David knew that the King would help him face this giant. The seed of greatness planted in David's heart now filled his entire body. All the weeds of discouragement that had been spoken to David were gone. The Kingdom seeds of strength and confidence now filled every inch of David. Lula lifted her sling shot and began to whirl it over her head. In the silence of the room, everyone could hear a hum as the sling shot went round and round. Goliath was angry that he was being challenged by puny little David with a sling shot. He hurled insults at David like lightning bolts.

Lula continued to whirl the slingshot around and around. At just the right moment she pretended to release the stone. Goliath, played by Todd the fire breathing dragon, fell onto the floor bouncing chairs like an earthquake. Everyone froze. Every eye was on Todd. After a long pause, Todd turned his head toward the kids and grinned the biggest grin ever and winked at Mary and Peter. Everyone in the room erupted in claps and cheers with high-five's everywhere.

From the back of the room staffers hurried in carrying large cardboard boxes. They began to stack them up and the kids realized they were building a giant cardboard Goliath. Goliath represented problems that were too big for the kids to manage on their own. Four staff members had to go up on the stage to place the final boxes. There stood Goliath painted on nine gigantic cardboard boxes over nine feet tall. His feet were on one box, then his legs on up to his head. Every kid there looked like a little grasshopper next to the cardboard Goliath.

Lula asked the kids and adults to name the weeds that had been planted in their hearts that were now the size of Goliath. Kids and staff named their giant weeds. The giant weeds of loneliness, fear, anger, sadness, rejection, hopelessness, and lots more. Then Lula invited anyone facing a giant-sized weed to come on stage and knock their weed down in the name of the King.

It was like popcorn over a hot fire. Kids from all over the room began to pop up and head toward the stage to take on their Goliath. Boys would do their best karate chop and let out a fierce "HI YAH" to defeat the Goliath

KRAK!!

sized weed of anger in their life.   As each boy looked at the Goliath painted on the boxes he would name the Goliath sized weed in his life. Down went fear. Down went rejection. Shouts of victory echoed around the room. Girls approached with their fists in the air and quick as a bunny hop they would hit Goliath with their best one two punches as they named their Goliath sized weeds. Goliath would wobble and then with one more solid punch down went more Goliath sized weeds of loneliness, sadness, and hopelessness. Shouts of pure joy filled every heart.

As each one approached the cardboard Goliath they said just what David said, "I come against you in the name of the King." At that moment everyone knew that no matter how big the problem was that they faced, the King was with them. Nothing was too big for the King! Kingdom seeds planted only five days ago had sprouted in hearts. Seeds of courage bloomed everywhere. A surprising number of seeds were already producing fruit as kids used their new courage to encourage others. Weeds had no chance against Kingdom seeds.

CHAPTER 11

HIDDEN POTENTIAL REVEALED

All week-long staff and campers had been preparing for this moment. "The World's Greatest Variety Show." Every day in the craft room costumes were being chosen. Rehearsals took place with songs selected, skits written, and talents practiced. Each one would take the stage and let the world see what extraordinary talent the King had planted inside them.

The room was filled with nervous energy. It felt like the first day of a new school year. One by one the acts were called to the stage. The same kids who were reluctant to get off the bus now boldly took the stage. There were singers, jugglers, piano players and more.

The same Daniel that had once sat by himself on the edge of the pool, now walked proudly beside Todd as a group of boys took the stage. Todd stood perfectly still while boys did flips off his head onto a small trampoline. Others climbed onto his tail and held on while Todd swung them back and forth. It was like gymnastics at the Olympics and Daniel scored another perfect "10."

Mary took the stage next. Todd's heart was beating so fast he thought he might faint. Mary began to read a poem she had written. The poem was about her giant weeds of fear and hopeless. Now she no longer wanted to hide and stay by herself. After a week at camp, she now had so many friends. The Kingdom seeds of courage and confidence had grown in Mary's heart and now she was sharing the Kingdom fruit with others. The giant weeds of loneliness and sadness were gone. It was amazing!

As Todd ran toward the stage, his weight caused the floor to bob up and down like waves on the ocean. Then he jumped up and down and shouted, "Mary, Mary." Everyone joined in. Todd went to the edge of the stage and bent down. Mary quickly climbed to the top of Todd's head. Todd and Mary led a parade around the room. As Mary climbed down Todd's back and took her seat, Todd noticed the curtain behind the stage move. Todd quietly made his way to the stage steps behind the curtain. Could this be whoever was trying to plant weeds? Todd would make sure whoever this was would be stopped.

One kid after another took the stage and brought down the house in loud applause. The hidden potential in each camper was now on full display. Peter was the last camper to take the stage. A hush fell over the room. Everyone remembered Peter the day he got off the bus.

Peter had thrown things at people and yelled. Everyone stayed away from him out of fear. Lula held her breath and almost fell off her chair. Could five days be long enough to change Peter forever? Lula took a deep breath and waited.

Peter invited all his new friends to come and sing his favorite camp song with him. Everyone ran to the stage. They all joined hands and began singing. Once no one wanted to be friends with Peter and now everyone was his friend. Kingdom seeds that had been planted in Peter all week long were growing in Peter's heart. The Variety Show ended and now it was time to go home. Everyone gathered up their things and got ready to leave.

Lula looked around for Todd and saw him motion for her to join him. Lula made her way over to the stage steps. She froze when she saw the stage curtain move. Now both Lula and Todd knew they might come face to face with whoever was trying to plant weeds. They were ready. Todd took hold of the curtain and pulled it back. Just as Todd pulled back the curtain, a girl ran full speed into his hand. She bounced back and landed flat on the floor. Lula and Todd were shocked! The girl laid on the floor and stared at Lula and Todd. Who was this girl and why was she behind the curtain? Could this girl be the one trying to plant weeds all week?

Lula now climbed up the stage steps and sat down beside the girl. Lula did not say a word and waited for the girl to speak. Instead of speaking the girl immediately began to cry. She said she was sorry for trying to plant weeds all week. She lived nearby the campground and every summer she watched kids have fun. She had never been allowed to come to camp. She wanted the kids to feel sad and lonely like she felt. She did not have friends and she did not want them to have friends. Her heart was overgrown with weeds of anger and jealousy. She wanted to know if it was possible for Kingdom seeds to be planted in her heart.

Todd and Lula immediately told her about the King and His love for her. They began planting Kingdom seeds of love into the girl that would root out the weeds. They told the girl the King had a limitless supply of Kingdom seeds. They would take her to meet the King. Lula motioned for the girl to follow her to the top of Todd's head. The three made their way outside.

As hard as it was to gather up their things and go home, every child knew Kingdom seeds would change their lives forever. They also knew to be on the lookout for weeds. Peter and Mary both had smiles and high-fives for everyone. All the kids were saying their goodbyes getting ready to get on the bus.

The staff was beginning to load up their things in cars, vans, trucks, and the bus. Before everyone left Lula and Todd got their attention. Lula told the staff and the kids that another girl was now part of the camp family.

Hugs and happy tears were everywhere. Everyone then gathered around the new little girl to tell her how excited they were for her to meet the King. Just then the sound of a trumpet blast split through the air. Everyone stopped in their tracks not knowing what was going on.

CHAPTER 12

UNEXPECTED VISITORS

The sound of a trumpet blasted through the trees calling everyone to attention. Just then every eye saw the King ride into camp on a powerful white horse. The horse's head was held high. Lula squealed and Todd let out a happy roar. The King was carried by their friend Majesty. Majesty had a bridle made of pure gold and his saddle was covered with precious jewels. Dazzling ribbons were woven into his tail. His hoofs shone like the sun at noontime. Golden bells around his neck chimed as he walked into camp.

The King wore a priceless purple robe. On the King's head sat His royal crown with large jewels surrounded by gold. The King's face was so brilliant it almost looked like a ball of fire. When the staff and kids looked on the King, they fell to their knees showing honor to the King.

What was going on? No one had expected the King

to ride into camp. Now it was completely silent. Even the birds had stopped singing. Majesty dropped to his knees and the King got down and walked toward them. Every human heart was beating well over the 60 -100 beats per minute normal for humans. Lula and Todd's hearts were racing. Then the King spoke. "I am proud of each and every one of you!" With those words a breeze blew through the campground. The birds began to sing. The staff began to sing and dance.

Professor Owl then flew in and sat on a branch in a nearby tree. Everyone grew quiet again not knowing what was happening. Were they supposed to leave? Was something else about to happen? Everyone stood perfectly still. Another hush fell over the camp.

The King told Todd to bring him a huge bag of seeds that Majesty was carrying on his saddle. The King took some seeds from the beautiful bag and spoke Mindy's name. Mindy dropped her clip board with her long-detailed plan and stood speechless. Lula was immediately at her side. The King stood with his scepter extended towards Mindy. Mindy shot a look at Professor Owl. Was she supposed to approach the King? Professor Owl nodded his head yes.

Mindy slowly made her way to the King. The King touched her shoulder gently with his scepter and spoke these words, "Well done Mindy. The seed of love I planted in your heart many years ago has grown, blossomed, and has now produced the fruit of love. Today I am planting more seeds of my love, courage, confidence into your heart." One by one the King called each staffer and camper by name to come to Him and He planted more Kingdom seeds in their hearts.

The King had called every name and had given them all more Kingdom seeds. Every name but one. Every eye was now focused on the new little girl. Then the King spoke the little girl's name. This was the first time anyone, including Lula and Todd, heard the little girl's name.

"Welcome Hazel. I love you, and I have been waiting for you."

Hazel walked toward the King. The King then held out His arms towards Hazel. When Hazel saw the King open His arms she ran to the King. He gathered her up into His arms. In that moment, the King planted more seeds of love in Hazel's heart and gave her a bag filled with all kinds of beautiful Kingdom seeds for her and more to plant in others. Hazel beamed! The camp erupted in joy.

Just then there was the sound of a monstrous dump truck making its way into the camp. Brian from the King's castle was behind the wheel. The dump truck pulled up right beside the King and stopped. With the push of a lever the dump truck bed began to slowly tilt upward. As the bed went higher and higher into the air, thousands and thousands of Kingdom seeds of every description began to pile up around Todd and Lula. Lula flew to the top of Todd's head where she would be safe. Todd began to climb the mountain of seeds.

Then the whole camp family began to climb the mountain of seeds. They filled their hands and pockets with seeds. They threw seeds into the air like glitter. Hazel jumped into the middle of the pile of seeds. Everyone now knew there was no lack of Kingdom seeds. They understood it was their choice to allow the King to plant Kingdom seeds into their life and then their turn to share Kingdom seeds with others. They could then trust the King to bring life from the seeds they would plant.

Suddenly Lula felt herself being hoisted up into the air. She quickly realized that Mindy had scooped her up and she now sat on Mindy's shoulder. Mindy ran straight for the dump truck. She yelled for Todd to jump in the back. Todd landed in the back of the truck just in time. The truck roared to life as Mindy sent gravel spraying through the air. Lula sat wide eyed on Mindy' shoulder. Mindy yelled for Lula to tell her how to get to the King's castle. Lula immediately squealed, "turn right at the next corner." Brian threw his head back and laughed.

Mindy just kept saying "I need more seeds. I need more seeds." Mindy's mind was already spinning as fast as an airplane propeller as she made plans for next year's camp. She wanted more than one dump truck filled with seeds. She wanted a fleet of trucks. Lula turned and looked at Todd as he sat in the back of the truck. Todd was making a very long list of seeds he wanted. Lula began shouting, "I need more Kingdom seeds. Turn left!"

At last Mindy spotted the giant sign reading, "Power Plant." She made a hard right-hand turn sending the truck up on two wheels. Todd bounced off the side of the truck bed and held on for dear life. Lula almost fainted. Before the truck came to a complete stop, Mindy jumped out. Todd was right behind her. Lula thought she would be safer with Todd and flew to the top of his head. As she was landing on Todd's head she spotted Nigel headed her way with an envelope in his mail pouch. Nigel swooped in like an eagle and placed the envelope in Lula's hand.

All three stopped in their tracks. Lula tore open the envelope and read, "Make sure you get seeds to take to the cement jungle." It was signed by the King. Mindy was now at the Power Plant door. Lula and Todd had no idea what the King meant by a cement jungle they just knew –

We Need More Kingdom Seeds!

We need
more seeds

THE KING LOVES YOU TOO!

"Welcome, ____________________. I love you, and I have been waiting for you."

I have chosen you to be my child. When you accept my invitation, you will live in my Kingdom of love. I cannot wait to spend time with you every day. We will talk about anything that makes you sad and share with each other what makes us laugh. If you need anything, you can come to me and ask. I will never leave you alone. I have great plans for your life. You never need to be afraid. Just call out to me for help and I am with you. Together we will face everything that concerns you.

Remember, I am not looking on the outside. I am looking at your beautiful heart. I saw you before you were born and beamed with pride. I saw you on your birthday, and I danced and sang with joy. You are my pride and joy!

So today, ______________ (date) we set out on a great adventure. Yes, some days may be scary, but I am with you. Yes, some days may be confusing to you, but remember I have a detailed plan for each day of your life. Trust me. Together we will fill each day to the brim with love and then let it overflow to everyone we meet.

Your life is the most valuable gift I have given you. The abundance you find in My Kingdom every day will be like Christmas as you go about giving out gifts of love, joy, peace, patience, kindness, goodness, faithfulness, gentleness, and self-control to everyone you meet.

Your loving Father, King Jesus

THE KING LOVES YOU TOO!